W9-BYA-407

Mary Blount Christian

SEBASTIAN
{Super Sleuth}
and the
Time Capsule
Caper

Illustrated by Lisa McCue

MACMILLAN PUBLISHING COMPANY
New York

COLLIER MACMILLAN PUBLISHERS
London

For Scott

JF
CAR

Macmillan Publishing Company
866 Third Avenue, New York, NY 10022
Collier Macmillan Canada, Inc.
First Edition
Printed in the United States of America

10 9 8 7 6 5 4 3 2 1

The text of this book is set in 12 point Primer.
The illustrations are rendered in scratchboard.

Library of Congress Cataloging-in-Publication Data
Christian, Mary Blount.
Sebastian (Super Sleuth) and the time capsule caper /
Mary Blount Christian; illustrated by Lisa McCue.—1st ed.
p.   cm.
Summary: Dog detective Sebastian investigates the
disappearance of the contents from a rich family's
sixty-year-old time capsule.
ISBN 0–02–718570–2
[1. Mystery and detective stories.   2. Dogs—Fiction.]
I. McCue, Lisa, ill.   II. Title.
III. Title: Time capsule caper.
PZ7.C4528Shc   1989   [Fic]—dc19   88–29295 CIP   AC

Contents

1
No Ball for Sebastian

Sebastian stopped scratching an itchy place behind his ear and leaned forward. He cocked one ear, listening to his human, John Quincy Jones.

John was on the phone, and although Sebastian could hear only half of what was being said, the cagey canine knew he was a good enough detective to figure out the other half.

John was a police detective and the only one of them actually earning a salary. But the hairy hawkshaw felt he, too, did *his* part to bring home the steak and potatoes (incidentally, his very favorite meal).

After all, it was he, Sebastian (Super Sleuth), who sniffed out clue after clue, sometimes having to stick them right under John's nose, he who was never satisfied until the perps were in jail. *Perps*—that's police talk for *perpetrators*, which means "criminals," Sebastian's mortal enemies.

Perhaps John was talking to Chief, their boss. Maybe Chief was giving them a new assignment!

Sebastian moved closer to the phone, wiggling with excitement. Crime-solving was in his blood!

"I picked up my costume at lunchtime yesterday," John was saying.

Sebastian sat up, more alert now. Costume? Was John going undercover? And why hadn't *he* been told?

"My costume?" John said. "It's really neat! The pants are kind of baggy, and there are gold buttons in two rows down the front of the coat. Mother found it in her attic and sent it to me. It was Grandfather Jones's. And I got a pair of brown and white shoes and a hat from the costume shop. The hat is a gas! I look like one of those gangsters from an old movie in it. Really perfect! This ball is going to be a lot of fun. What a great idea to have a nineteen twenties costume ball to unseal the time capsule!"

Costume ball? So it wasn't a case, after all. Still, nobody had invited *him* to any ball! Why hadn't he been told about it? An oversight, surely. And *what* time capsule? Fail to read the papers for a few days, and what happens? The world goes on without you! *Humpt.*

"I'll pick you up about seven, Maude. Bet you'll look terrific in those clothes." John hung up, whistling.

Maude! So it was John's girlfriend he'd been talking to. Just listen to him, whistling one of those dumb songs about love and marriage and junk like that. Sebastian hoped John wasn't getting stupid ideas!

Happy as a puppy with a new toy, John was. Shoot! Sebastian guessed John planned on going to the costume ball without him, with *her* instead. Well, fat chance! He'd find out all about that ball. Nobody, but nobody, withheld information from the four-on-the-floor sleuth!

Sebastian was sure the newspapers would have had an article about such an event. He trotted into the kitchen and rummaged through the old newspapers John had stacked by the garbage pail. He found the story he was looking for.

TIME CAPSULE TO BE UNSEALED
AT COSTUME BALL FRIDAY EVENING

The story claimed that everybody who was anybody would attend. *Humpt.* Little did they realize!

It seemed the time capsule had been planted in the cornerstone of the VanderVanden Building in November of 1929, when it was built. Although the VanderVanden family later sold the building, the personal possessions donated by each of the children remained in the cornerstone. There were three VanderVanden children: Vanita was twelve, Van III was ten, and Vanoise was six. A picture of the children showed them making faces at the camera. They looked angry. Was it because they hadn't wanted to put their things in the cornerstone?

3

The building was sold several times over the years, most recently to the city, which used it for the water and tax departments. Then the city council voted to tear down the building to make room for a new glass and steel library.

Nearly all the family members protested bitterly and sued the city in an effort to block the demolition. But they lost the court battle, and the building was finally torn down. However, the time capsule they'd planted was salvaged, and the mayor planned to auction off the contents.

Mayor Theresa Bellows decided that the time capsule would be opened publicly during a big celebration and that the contents would then be auctioned off to help pay for the new library. "This will be a gala event for the city," she told the newspaper. "We will celebrate the future by auctioning off the past. The time capsule will be under guard until the opening during the ball," the mayor concluded.

There was a current picture, too, of the mayor, a security guard, and the capsule. Sebastian studied the picture. It didn't look like a capsule at all! It looked more like a box—a rusty metal box about the size of a lunch box, with a padlock. It appeared that the padlock had wax on it where the loop snapped into the hole. An indentation in the wax probably had been made by a ring or special seal. The story explained that Van VanderVanden I had used his own signet ring to make the indentation.

The article went on to name the items left in the time capsule: pewter toy soldiers, an alabaster toothpick holder, a streetcar token from that year, Victorian-era paper dolls, a glass *millefiori* ("many flowers") paperweight, cat's-eye marbles, and even a dime minted that year. It all sounded pretty much like junk to Sebastian, who expected such a rich family to throw in at least a few pieces of jewelry or gold.

The article also said that while the VanderVanden family members shared the ownership of a department store, other buildings, and a mansion, they did not speak to one another. There was more, but Sebastian decided not to finish the article then. Instead he ripped it from the paper and tucked it neatly under his water bowl for safekeeping.

"Sebastian!" John's voice roaring from the living room made him jump. "Did I hear you tearing up paper again?" John appeared in the doorway. "What are you doing in the garbage? What a mess! Shame, Sebastian!" John hastily restacked the papers.

Sebastian trotted haughtily from the kitchen. Not ask *him* to such an important event, huh? Well, he'd show his human! He would go to tonight's costume ball, invitation or not. But where would he get a costume at this late hour?

2
Oh, for a Fairy Dogmother

Cinderella had had a fairy godmother to help her get a new outfit for the ball. Alas, Sebastian would have to take care of himself. Well, Cinderella wasn't a noble canine with an ingenious mind!

Clever and cagey as he was, Sebastian knew just what to do. And since John, who was off work today, had rushed out to pick up the corsage he'd ordered for Maude, the coast was clear.

Sebastian rummaged through the clutter on John's dresser and found his plastic charge card. Holding it carefully in his mouth so he wouldn't accidentally mar it with a toothprint and make it useless, he dashed out through the doggie door and down the street to his favorite costume shop. Scooting in unnoticed, he scanned the racks of hangers. A Confederate soldier's uniform, a Southern belle outfit, a palace guard's uniform. Ah, perfect! He shimmied into the dark blue constable's uniform with its rows of shiny silver buttons and badge. He dislodged the helmet from the rack and it plopped onto his head. To all the world, he would be an old-time cop!

Sebastian dropped the charge card on the counter, and the clerk filled out the rental slip. "Going to the twenties costume ball, huh?" he said as he shoved the rental slip toward Sebastian.

"*Huh-huh,*" Sebastian panted. When the man had turned his back to straighten a rack of clothes, Sebastian snatched the pen between his teeth and made something like an X on the dotted line. He brushed the charge card into the costume pocket and dashed out the door.

Sebastian reached the convention center a bit early. The ball wouldn't start for another hour, at least. The front entrance was still locked, and a guard was posted outside the door. Without an invitation, he doubted he could get in like everyone else, anyway.

Sebastian spotted a group of fellows in twenties-style costumes, carrying musical instruments. He followed them into the convention center's alley, where they entered through a side door. A guard motioned them inside. Maybe if he pretended to be a musician, he could get in, too.

Sebastian fell in behind the last musician, who was carrying a bass fiddle on his back. Just as he was about to go in, the guard put a large hand on his shoulder.

"Hold it! You don't look like a musician to me. Where's your musical instrument? You trying to sneak in?"

Sebastian opened his mouth to protest, but all that came out was a sorrowful howl. *"Oooooooooooo."*

"Oh, sorry," the guard said, "the singer, huh? You sound just like that Michael Jackson. Go ahead."

Sebastian dipped his head in a gesture of appreciation and trotted in.

The huge ballroom was decorated with old dome-shaped radios and pictures of some guy singing into a megaphone, planes with four wings, and people all dressed up and doing funny-looking dances. The article he'd been reading earlier had been blown up to an enormous size and pinned to one wall. Another article, dated November 6, 1929, was next to it. The blowups were so big that Sebastian could read the articles from across the room.

A stage, decorated in streamers and balloons, had a white, satin-draped table at its center. A spotlight flooded the table, on which there was a lump under more satin. That lump must be the metal box that everyone was calling the time capsule. A uniformed guard stood nearby. A huge mirror had been hung at an angle above the stage so people could get a good view of the top of the box.

Television and newspaper reporters and photographers, perhaps twelve in all, were fighting one another for the best spot from which to take pictures of the capsule. The guard wouldn't let them get too near it. "That's close enough!" he commanded, holding up one hand for emphasis. "I don't want any more incidents with this thing."

"More! You said *more* incidents," a tall woman in a gray suit said. She shoved a microphone toward him. "Have there been others? What incidents?"

Sebastian's ears wiggled under his hat. Their conversation had caught his attention. He moved closer to listen.

"Well," the guard said, "there was an incident just a little while ago, at five o'clock, when the lights went out for a few minutes. Somebody must've shut off the fuse box by mistake, or perhaps too many electrical items were plugged in. No one knows for sure. But we stood guard through it all. The capsule remained right here the whole time."

"We?" the woman said.

The guard cleared his throat. "Yes, ma'am, at five o'clock a guard came to relieve me. I was not familiar with him, and I had just begun to work. Following the policy of my employer, the Stan Appleton Security Agency, I asked for identification. Then the lights went out, and neither of us could see a thing.

"The other security guard offered to stay with the time capsule while I checked the fuse box. I declined to leave my post, since it was still officially my shift. He agreed that I should stay with the capsule, and he went to see about the fuse box. In a few moments, the lights came back on. I guess he found the trouble, although he didn't come back to tell me exactly what it was."

Since that "incident," as the security guard called it, was not very spectacular and certainly didn't lend itself to visual effects, the reporters shut off their cameras and put away their notebooks. They scattered to other parts of the floor, looking for somebody else to interview.

Sebastian thought it was a good time to look for something more interesting, too. Along one long wall of the room were tables with lace tablecloths and tapered white candles in branched silver candleholders. Where there were tables, there was probably food, too. Yummy! It reminded Sebastian that he hadn't eaten in an hour, maybe two. He trotted over to investigate.

Near the tables were serving carts filled with stacks of silver platters and stainless steel food warmers covered with high silver domes. If Sebastian's nose served him correctly (and usually it did), they contained roast beef, ham, and vegetables drenched in rich sauces. The waiters were lighting little fat candles under the pans to keep the food hot, and they were putting out silver platters of little sandwiches.

As soon as they'd finished, Sebastian slurped up a half dozen sandwiches, then slipped under the table. He was sure they wouldn't approve of one of the "musicians" eating.

The lace tablecloth allowed him to see out but hid him very well. It was fairly dark under the table, and it seemed like a good place to stay until the guests started arriving. He was much less likely to be noticed in a crowd.

Everywhere Sebastian looked, the waiters and waitresses, men and women in white shirts and gloves and black trousers and vests, bustled around, setting up the buffet supper. "Those VanderVandens are an odd lot, aren't they?" one of them said in a decidedly British accent. Sebastian could reach out and touch the waiter's feet, he was so close. He hunkered into a furry ball and peered up through the cloth at the man.

The man was nearly six feet tall and of average build. His thick black hair and short brush mustache showed no trace of gray, although he definitely had the jowls of an older man.

Perhaps he dyed his hair and mustache, Sebastian thought. Or maybe he even wore a toupee. Sebastian snickered to himself. Humans were so vain! Of course, they didn't have as much going for them as canines.

The waiter's brown eyes seemed always to watch the waitress as she pulled the warming pans from the carts and placed them on the table. "No, not that warmer. It didn't smell right and should be returned unopened." He nodded approvingly. "Yes, that's fine. Just leave it. As I was saying, those Vander-Vandens are always bickering amongst themselves, from what I hear."

"If that warmer of food is spoiled, you'd better tell the security guard, then," the young woman said, obviously choosing to ignore his gossip. "I'm pretty sure it's the one you rolled over earlier so you could give him a bit of food before the reporters came in."

"You must be mistaken," the man said. "As I was saying, fighting the city to save that building is about the only thing they've ever agreed on, it seems. Why, they rarely speak to each other, except by memo or a third person. Or so I hear."

"I'd rather not talk about them, if you don't mind," said the woman, who seemed to be in her early thirties. "And are you sure about the beef? I could've sworn you were pushing that cart. Remember how it squeaked?"

"Forget it, please," the waiter said. He sounded cross. "I'll take care of it. Just do your job."

She sighed. "Why do I have to be here tonight?"

"Yes, yes, why indeed," he said, pulling some silverware and napkins from a box. "You said your name was Vanessa, didn't you?" the man asked. "And your last name is Vander*something,* isn't it? Wouldn't it be a pip if *you* could say you were kin to them? You'd have a share of all that money!" He laughed.

"Yeah," the woman said. "Hilarious. I just don't happen to think money is all that important. Oh, no! It's *her*!" She shrieked.

The tablecloth fluttered, and suddenly Sebastian

found himself face to face with the young woman in the waitress uniform. She had crawled under the table, too!

Strawberry blond hair spilled out from the chef's cap on her head, and she hastened to tuck it back in. From her expression, she was as surprised to see Sebastian as he was to see her. Her emerald green eyes widened, and she put a finger to her lips, signaling him to be quiet. Sebastian glanced at the plastic pin on her vest. It said "Vanessa."

Rhinestone-studded shoes and the hem of a sequined dress appeared next to the table where the two were hiding. "Where is that waitress who was here a moment ago?" a woman demanded in sharp tones.

Vanessa cringed and once again motioned for Sebastian to be silent—as if he were about to give himself away!

The waiter who'd been talking before sounded flustered. "Er, uh, she was just here, ma'am. Is there something wrong?"

Sebastian wondered the same thing. Why *was* the waitress hiding?

"She looked quite familiar," the woman said. "But, no, of course not. A niece of *mine* would *never* work here. Tragic enough that she left her wonderful home, that at her age she wanted to go to school and learn something *useful,* to—" She laughed. "No, that's ridiculous. It must have been someone who

only *looked* like her."

The rhinestone-studded shoes disappeared, and Sebastian and Vanessa both let out sighs of relief. As a squeaking sound gradually faded, she peered through the cloth. "Good, that nosy old waiter is taking the spoiled food out to the catering van. Now's my chance." She smiled at Sebastian, said, "Thanks," and slid out from their hiding place.

She'd been right that the cart was squeaky, Sebastian noted. He stayed a few moments longer. Finally, when the ballroom had begun to fill up, he slipped out from under the table and pushed into the crowd, keeping his eyes open for John and *her.*

The band was now playing twenties tunes, and the people wiggled and jumped and swung their bodies to the rhythm. Sebastian thought they looked as if they were trying to scratch fleas. Spotting John with Maude, the hairy hawkshaw made his way through the crowd until he got close enough to hear their conversation.

"Look at that costume, John," Maude said. "Isn't he cute?"

Sebastian realized she was looking at him! She certainly had better taste than he'd imagined.

"Of course, not as cute as you, John," Maude added. She gazed into his eyes and sighed.

Yuk! Maude and John were looking at each other the same way Sebastian looked at a thick sirloin steak. This couldn't be good!

John grinned at Maude. "And you, Maude, you look absolutely gorgeous!"

Oh, no! Sebastian thought. Next thing you knew, John would be asking Maude to marry him! He'd better do something quick.

Maude dipped her head and smiled. "It was my grandmother's *wedding* gown. Every bead was hand sewn by her. She saved it for me . . . for someday, she said."

John had a stupid look on his face that worried Sebastian. "Which brings me to something I've been intending—"

Like an oncoming bus, Sebastian hurled himself at John as hard as he could. Not very original, he realized, but it was the best he could do on such short notice.

"Oh!" John cried out, and bumped into Maude.

"Oh!" Maude wailed as she bumped into someone else and her string of pearls broke, scattering like raindrops across the dance floor. Couples were slipping and sliding as if they were on roller skates, until at least a dozen people lay sprawled all over the dance floor.

"Attention, out there!" someone on the microphone yelled as the people struggled to their feet and began gathering pearls. The band hit a loud note. "Attention!"

Uh-oh. Sebastian slunk off, hangdog, into the crowd. He was in trouble now!

3
Surprises Come in Small Packages

Sebastian slipped farther into the crowd, cringing behind a large man. He might be in trouble, but it was worth it if he'd kept John from asking Maude to marry him.

But, thank goodness, the announcer wasn't after Sebastian. He introduced the band, The Twenty-Niners, then paused while the drummer executed a drum roll that ended with a clash of cymbals. "We've all been waiting for this special moment," the announcer said. "And here is Mayor Theresa Bellows to explain what we are about to do."

Mayor Bellows took the microphone. "In a moment, I will break open the seal on the time capsule, and the auctioneer will open the bidding on the individual items. We have already had a bid of one hundred thousand dollars for the unopened capsule from Van VanderVanden III, who placed his own toy soldiers there when he was a young boy. That is certainly a generous offer, but you folks have to have a chance, too." With a flourish, she snatched the satin cover off the box. "Am I right?"

The crowd let out a big cheer and applauded.

The mayor then called for an assistant to hand her the gold-plated chisel and hammer. She leaned over the metal box and placed the chisel on the lock. She tapped it once, twice. The wax sealer fell away, and the lock snapped open.

There was another drum roll and clash of cymbals as the mayor flung open the box. The crowd cheered and stomped their feet excitedly.

Suddenly the mayor shrieked. Recovering her composure, she returned to the microphone. "We— we've been *robbed*! The time capsule is empty!"

Sebastian glanced at the mirror that hung above. She was right. The box lay open and was completely empty.

Quickly John pulled his badge from his pocket and held it above his head. Using his other hand to pull Maude through the crowd with him, he made his way toward the stage. "Let me through, please," he kept repeating. "Police officer. Let me through, please."

Fortunately for Sebastian, he was able to squirm and wiggle through the forest of legs a lot faster than John, and he reached the time capsule first. Sure enough, not even a lint ball inside.

Before the hairy hawkshaw had time to study it properly, though, John called for a tablecloth and threw it over the box. "To avoid further fingerprints

21

until the lab boys get a chance to go over it," he explained to the mayor.

She nodded, smiling her approval. "It's all yours, Detective Jones."

John stepped quickly to the microphone. "Secure the doors immediately," he instructed. "No one is to leave here until you have given your name, address, and statement to an officer. Any off-duty officers here, raise your hands." He nodded as about four hands shot into the air. (Sebastian kept his paw down; he figured he'd be more effective undercover.)

"You," John said, pointing to a woman in a blue beaded dress, "take the front entrance. And you take the back," he told a man in a dark blue suit. "You," he said to another, "call downtown and get some help in here quick." He motioned to the remaining man. "You check to see that there's no way to get out through the rest rooms."

The mayor nodded and turned to the crowd, one arm raised above her head in a triumphant gesture. "When I came into office, I promised a strengthened police force. Now you are seeing our city's finest at work. We will investigate this terrible theft thoroughly."

Sebastian opened his mouth in a wide, panting grin. This would certainly take John's mind off Maude—and marriage. There was nothing like a good mystery to occupy the mind!

The mayor motioned to the band, which began

playing again. "Now, please, as soon as you've given your name and address to the officers, continue with the dance," she told the people. "Let's not allow a thief to rob us of a good time, too!"

Some of the people danced, but others stood gawking at the stage, speculating about the robbery.

John turned to the security guard, who was still standing with his mouth open, staring at the lump the box made under the tablecloth. "And I'll want to talk to you and the other guards. So don't leave, understand?"

Maude tapped John on the shoulder. "Is there anything I can do to help, John?" She was looking at John with that silly goo-goo-eyed expression she sometimes got around him.

John shrugged. "Give your name and address to the officer, Maude. It wouldn't do for someone to think you were getting special treatment. Then you can just wander around and eavesdrop. Let me know if you hear anything relevant to the case."

Humpt! Sebastian thought. This was no time for civilians, especially *that* civilian, to get in the way of an investigation! Well, if it kept John from asking Maude to marry him, he guessed it would be all right. Sebastian sure didn't want to share his home with Maude and her ditzy dog, Lady Sharon.

"Maybe later we can talk, okay?" John told Maude.

Yes, later. The later the better, as far as Sebastian was concerned.

When Maude had wandered over to give one of the officers her name and address, John asked the mayor, "Can you tell me if the capsule has been under guard the entire time?"

"Absolutely," the mayor said. "The Stan Appleton Security Agency has handled it." She looked away, obviously embarrassed. "We didn't feel there was any need to guard it, but Mr. Appleton offered to do so for free. He thought it would be good publicity for his agency. And it seemed like good publicity for the fund-raising auction, too. No one ever seriously thought the capsule was in danger. If I had, I'd have involved the police force."

Hmmm, Sebastian thought. If Stan Appleton had volunteered his services, maybe it was to give himself a chance to steal the time capsule. But why would he endanger his agency's reputation for these trinkets?

Mayor Bellows leaned away from the microphone and spoke in almost a whisper. Sebastian had to strain to hear. "Even if the time capsule had been in danger, I would have hesitated to use our police force. You know Rogers would have accused me of being frivolous with city money and personnel." She sighed wearily. "Now he'll be accusing me of failing to provide adequate security, I suppose. It's a no-win situation."

John poised his pencil over his notebook. "Rogers, Mayor?"

She laughed slightly. "Either you are one of my supporters or you haven't the slightest interest in politics."

Where had John been lately? Sebastian chuckled under his breath. Patrick Rogers was already running for mayor, even though the race was six months away. Sebastian had seen his commercials on television.

If losing the goods in the time capsule that had been committed to her care might help defeat the mayor in a race, her opponent certainly had a motive for taking them. That would make Rogers a suspect worth investigating. Sebastian didn't recall seeing him at the costume ball tonight, however.

Mayor Bellows turned around to face a short, round man who'd come to the stage. "Mr. Appleton, will you please acquaint Detective Jones with your security procedures for the time capsule?"

Mr. Appleton was a red-faced man with piercing, ice blue eyes. He looked straight at John as he spoke. "Two of my guards were on the scene when the time capsule was extracted from the cornerstone several months ago. That is well documented by the newspapers and television coverage.

"From there the time capsule was placed in one of our armored trucks and carried to the Van-Mart store downtown."

Sebastian narrowed his eyes, thinking. The newspaper article had said the VanderVandens owned a department store. With a name like Van-Mart, surely it belonged to them. Had one of them gotten the mayor to stash the time capsule at that store, giving him—or her—a better opportunity to steal what was inside it?

Mr. Appleton continued. "At that time it was secured in a store-front window. It was on view twenty-four hours a day and constantly guarded until four o'clock today, when the object was transported to this location."

So the time capsule had been brought here at 4:00 P.M. The guard had said there was "an incident" at 5:00 P.M. If the culprit was a VanderVanden, perhaps he—or she—had failed to break into the capsule at the store and tried again here.

John's eyes narrowed as he studied Mr. Appleton's face. "At no time was the capsule left unguarded?"

The man looked straight into John's eyes and squared his jaw stubbornly. "At no time! With all the publicity this time capsule has generated, I'd be a fool not to be absolutely sure that nothing happened to it." He blushed and stared at his feet, clearing his throat.

Sebastian nodded in agreement. Of course, if the capsule really hadn't been tampered with since its uncovering, that would mean it had been buried empty.

Was he dealing with a contemporary crime, or with one that had taken place sixty years ago?

4
Those VanderVandens!

Sebastian trotted over to a corner of the ballroom, trying to sort through what he knew so far—and what he *didn't* know. The metal box that they called a time capsule had been sealed inside a cornerstone for sixty years. Since being removed, it had been under guard. Yet when the box was opened, it was empty.

There were several possibilities. One, of course, was that it had been empty all these years, part of a hoax by the VanderVanden parents, although he could think of no reason why they would do such a thing. Or perhaps it had been a prank by the VanderVanden children. Maybe now they were embarrassed by it and sought to cover it up.

Another possibility was that the contents had been stolen while the capsule was in the hands of the Appleton Security Agency. But that seemed unlikely. No, he would focus on that Rogers fellow and the VanderVandens themselves.

Sebastian peered out from his dark corner of the

ballroom. The police reinforcements had arrived, and they were beginning to divide up the people for the interviews. He tried to look casual as he wandered about, eavesdropping on them.

He did find that there were a number of collectors and investors at the ball, eager to bid on the different items. Far from being junk, which he'd first thought them, the pewter soldiers, if a full set and in mint condition, might go for as much as $3,000. The paper dolls, if undamaged, might sell for $750. The alabaster toothpick holder could bring $1,500. And the cat's-eye marbles could sell for $100 each. The paperweight, described as a *millefiori*, might sell for $2,300.

Suddenly Sebastian was aware that one of the police officers was motioning to him!

"You," the officer said. "What's your name?"

Sebastian kept his head low so that his helmet would hide his face. He had seen the officer many times in the station and didn't want to take a chance on being recognized. "*Arrrp!*" A bark escaped his fuzzy lips.

"Arp, you say?" the officer asked. He turned around. "All the rest of you, A through C, fall in line behind Mr. Arp." Turning back to Sebastian, he asked, "First name?"

"*Rrrrrrr,*" Sebastian growled.

"Roy Arp. Okay. Did you see anyone hanging around the stage, other than the guard?"

"*Hunt, hunt,*" Sebastian panted, almost too afraid to say anything.

"Uh-uh? No, Mr. Arp? Okay, Mr. Arp," the officer said. "But hang around in case we need to ask you anything else. I'll just put this little red sticker on your costume. That will show the other officers that you've already given your name to me, and you'll be free to dance or wander around or even leave, if you wish."

Fat chance he'd leave before solving this caper! Sebastian, grateful that he'd managed to fool the police officer, figured he shouldn't push his luck too far. He saw a door marked Rest Rooms. That meant there would be a hallway, where he could hide a few moments and gather his thoughts. He dashed into the hallway and collided straightaway with a trash barrel.

Paper towels and napkins and paper plates spilled to the floor. Wait a minute. What was that tucked away among the towels? Something black.

Sebastian dug at the papers, sending them flying in all directions. It was the jacket to a uniform identical to those worn by the security guards of Stan Appleton's group. The gold buttons were engraved SASA for Stan Appleton Security Agency, but one was missing from the jacket pocket. And there was a roast beef stain on the jacket.

Odd that it would be discarded in a trash barrel in the hallway outside the rest rooms. Couldn't it be

mended and cleaned? And where were the trousers?

What was that odd stain around the collar? Makeup! Had the thief used a security guard uniform to get to the time capsule? Makeup on the collar certainly pointed to a woman. But which woman? Half the people here tonight were women. Or might the smear be there because the guard had been dancing cheek to cheek with a woman? Sebastian dismissed that idea. It was impossible for a guard on duty to be dancing. Besides, this stain was more on the *inside* edge of the collar, as if it had been rubbed from a neck.

He nudged the paper towels back over the uniform and pushed until he had the garbage pail upright. The jacket might have a simple explanation, although he could think of none right now. Or it might belong to the mystery guard who'd shown up for the wrong shift. At this point Sebastian wasn't sure what significance it had, and he didn't want to tip his paw by calling it to John's attention just yet.

Sebastian figured if he stayed near the interviews, he might pick up a few valuable clues. He saw Maude circulating through the crowd, and he certainly didn't want her to beat him to a clue. He wandered onto the dance floor again and ambled among the people. They were being interviewed, one by one, in alphabetical order.

Sebastian headed toward the line of people behind a crude sign that said Q–Z, moving casually so as not to call attention to himself. It seemed strange, alphabetizing the suspects like that, but it was probably the only way to handle so many people at once. It certainly would help him to locate all the VanderVandens quickly.

Suddenly there was a terrible commotion as a raucous alarm went off. One of the police officers was holding onto a struggling, shrieking person in dark trousers and vest. The chef's hat fell off, and strawberry blond hair tumbled to her shoulders.

"Let me go! I said, let me go!" she demanded shrilly. "I know my rights!" It was Vanessa, the young woman who'd shared a hiding place with him earlier.

John ran over to see what was the matter. "This one was trying to get away, Detective Jones," the police officer said. "She set off the alarm when she tried to sneak out through the fire exit."

"I didn't do it!" she insisted. "I didn't!"

Why would she be trying to sneak out if she wasn't guilty? Sebastian searched her face for a clue to what she was thinking. Had the thief been caught already?

5

Here a VanderVanden, There a VanderVanden

Sebastian, careful to keep out of John's line of vision, trotted over near the exit to listen. While it was not likely, it *was* possible that some day John might recognize him. These little challenges were part of the excitement, though.

"But I don't want to be here! I don't know anything at all, honest!" Vanessa told John. She struggled to loose herself from the officer's grip. "I know my rights."

"Then you don't know them very well," John said, taking her by the arm and leading her to a corner. He instructed the officer to keep the news reporters and cameras away. "No one is accusing you of stealing the capsule contents, miss—not yet, anyway," he told Vanessa. "But it's possible that you're at least a material witness to a crime, and your very presence makes you a suspect. We're certainly within *our* rights to question you."

The crowd of people was staring at them, and the young woman seemed almost to shrink so that John was between her and the crowd. "Please don't let them look at me," she whispered. "I didn't see anything. Really!"

John smiled, obviously trying to reassure her. "Miss, if you'll just calm down, we'll get this over with in a hurry. As one of the waitresses, you were here earlier than most of us. Think, now. Perhaps you saw something but didn't realize it was part of a crime. We are certainly not accusing you of anything criminal, Miss—Ms.—?"

"Ms. Ms. Vanessa VanderVanden," she whispered. Her emerald green eyes were wide with fright.

"What was that?" John asked. "Did you say VanderVanden?"

"Shhhh," Vanessa pleaded. "I don't want *them*—"

From the Q–Z line, Vanita VanderVanden gasped. "I knew it! I knew it! It *was* Vanessa. Oh, how tragic! She is working like a—an ordinary person!" She fanned herself and turned to the people in line behind her. "Tell my brother I told him so. That is, I would have if I were speaking to him. After all, it's *his* daughter! Oh, I think I'm going to faint."

The crowd moved over a couple of feet, giving Vanita plenty of room to fall. She moved over, too, then flopped onto the floor, moaning.

A man with emerald eyes and streaks of gray in his strawberry blond hair said, "Tell my sister to stop being such a phony." He threw a glass of water on her.

She shrieked and came up flailing her arms. "Tell my brother that was a sixty-dollar coiffure he ruined! And look at my dress!"

The man with gray streaks laughed. "And tell my sister her sixty-dollar coiffure looks like a six-dollar wig. As for that dress . . ."

A very old bald man with the same green eyes waved his gold-handled cane. "Somebody tell my son and my daughter to stop their bickering this minute! I'd tell them so myself, if I were speaking to either of them!"

"*Arrrrrg,*" Vanessa said to John. "*That*'s why I didn't want them to know I was here. They drive me *crazy,* always fighting, fighting, fighting! Never speaking to each other, just *around* each other."

Of all the VanderVandens, Sebastian liked Vanessa best. He would be very disappointed if she turned out to be the thief.

Sebastian did notice that Vanessa's trousers were similar in color and style to those of the security guards. With a jacket over the vest and shirt, it would look enough like the guards' uniform to fool all but those as observant as he. With some sort of disguise, perhaps dark glasses, a false nose, a wig, mustache, that sort of thing, who knows? Perhaps she had passed as a guard and stolen the contents. But how?

35

Sebastian wanted to believe it was someone else who'd stolen the capsule contents. He and Vanessa had shared a hiding place together. And she hadn't told on him. She had nice eyes, too, direct and honest. Sebastian felt he could tell a lot about humans from their eyes.

"I'm trying to make it on my own," Vanessa told John once he had calmed down the other VanderVandens. "They don't approve of my working at all, let alone working as a waitress. And I'm finally putting myself through college. I figure it's never too late."

John checked his notebook. "Let's see, now. I have you, Vanessa VanderVanden, and your aunt, Vanita VanderVanden. Then there's your father, Van VanderVanden III, and your grandfather, Van VanderVanden II, right?"

Vanessa nodded.

"Is that all the VanderVandens?" John asked.

"No," Vanessa said.

"Yes," the other VanderVandens said at the same time.

"Which is it?" John asked. "Are there more VanderVandens or not?"

Sebastian edged closer, remembering the article. If John had read it, as *he* had, he'd know that there were three VanderVanden children. So where was the third one?

Vanessa said, "It's yes, a definite yes, no matter

36

what the others say. Uncle Vanoise VanderVanden was disinherited by my grandfather because he wanted to be an actor—"

"Thespian," Vanita VanderVanden said. "Tell her if she must talk about that person at all, the word is *thespian.*"

Vanessa rolled her emerald eyes and made a face. "Whatever you want to call it. When he went on the stage in 1943, he was disinherited. And my father will disinherit me, too." She sighed wistfully. "And, furthermore, I don't care. I love them, really I do, but my family are such snobs, I'm sorry to say."

Sebastian hated to even think it, but if Vanessa was about to be disinherited, she certainly had a motive for stealing valuable articles that could be sold for good money. He gave a wistful sigh. What about the uncle? He sifted through his computerlike memory, searching for that most unusual name. He didn't recall ever seeing the name Vanoise VanderVanden on a theater marquee.

"I don't remember ever seeing your uncle act," John said, echoing Sebastian's concerns.

"He changed his name to Van Hamlet," Vanessa said. "That's one reason the family is so angry with him. But I'm sure they'd be angrier if he'd kept the family name when he went on the stage." She smiled. "I slipped in to see him one time. He was wonderful! He played three parts in the play, and each character looked and sounded different. He's an absolute *master* of disguise."

Vanita VanderVanden stepped forward, eyebrows raised haughtily. "Tell *her* that we are disappointed that she went to the theater to see *that person*. We VanderVandens do not wish to see *that person* again." Her emerald green eyes snapped with anger.

"Oh, pooh!" Vanessa said. She turned to John. "See what I mean? Aren't they a drag?"

Her aunt harumphed and turned her back to Vanessa and John.

Van VanderVanden III was just as strange. He wouldn't look at Vanita or Vanessa. "Tell *her*," he said, looking past Vanessa, "that I am horrified that she won't come home and do nothing like the rest of us. It's a VanderVanden tradition."

"But, Daddy—"

"And tell her that I don't wish to *speak* to her until she comes home where she belongs. And furthermore, if the city had accepted my bid of one hundred thousand dollars for the unopened capsule, we wouldn't be standing here waiting to be interviewed by the police like common criminals."

Sebastian wondered if that was something of a confession. Was Van VanderVanden III saying that because the city wouldn't let him buy the capsule's contents, he'd *stolen* them? Or was he only saying that had he been able to buy them, they wouldn't have been available for theft?

Vanita VanderVanden turned her nose in the

air. "And tell *him* that if he stole the time capsule material, he should give me back my paper dolls and my alabaster toothpick holder."

John looked from one VanderVanden to another. "She said—"

"And you can tell *her* for me that I don't have the stuff. But she can give back my miniature pewter soldiers."

"And the 1929 streetcar token, although I hasten to add that I personally have never ridden a streetcar," the elder Van VanderVanden said.

"Tell my father and my brother that I don't have any of those things," Vanita said.

The VanderVandens, two generations of them, went on arguing about trinkets that had been locked away for sixty years.

So far, Vanessa was the only VanderVanden Sebastian thought he might like at all. But he couldn't dismiss her as a suspect. After all, she came to this ball, she tried to hide her identity, and she had been here early enough to have taken the material from the box. That is, *if* it was a modern crime and not one committed long ago.

If the crime had taken place in 1929, then Vanessa would be the only VanderVanden who was not suspect. She wouldn't have been born yet!

Harumpt! Something between a grizzly's growl and a thunderclap made Sebastian—and John, too, he noted—jump. It was the big bad wolf!

6
Who's Afraid of the Big Bad Wolf?

The growl and the grumpy face belonged to Chief, John's boss. Obviously he had been informed about the theft, and about John's being in charge here, and had rushed down to the convention center to grumble at him. Fortunately for Sebastian, Chief did not know *he* was there.

"Well, I might have known something dreadful would happen if *you* were around, Detective Jones," Chief said, edging toward one of the buffet tables as he spoke. He piled a few chicken puffs and a half dozen finger sandwiches on a plate, pausing to stuff a couple into his mouth. *"Mummmmph, mlug.* Don't you realize that you are a police officer twenty-four hours a day, Jones? Couldn't you be more alert and do a little preventive policing?"

Sebastian curled his lip, growling under his breath. Blaming John for this! The very idea! He should have been here when John took control of the situation earlier. Sebastian had been downright proud of him. He couldn't have done better himself.

While Chief was ranting about John's handling of the case, Sebastian edged close enough to Chief's plate to gulp down the sandwiches and puffs. Delicious!

"Wha—?" Chief yelled. "What happened to my sandwiches? You didn't bring that flea bag of a walking garbage gobbler with you tonight, did you?"

"Why, of course not, Chief. You know this is for people only. As for the sandwiches, you must have eaten them, Chief," John said.

"Humpft! Yes, well," Chief muttered. "I suppose I've had enough, then. Must watch the old diet, you know." He licked his lips as if testing to see for himself. "Well, get on with this thing, John! Get all the evidence you can before we have to let these people go home!"

John snapped almost to attention. "Right, Chief! It's practically solved!"

If John knew, he was ahead of Sebastian. And that would certainly be a switch. The clever old canine figured John was only saying that to get Chief off his back.

Chief left John to go to the buffet table again, and Sebastian would bet that John was just as glad as he. At that moment one of the police officers in charge of searching the building for the capsule contents reported to John. "We've searched the whole

41

building, and we didn't find the contents as described, sir. But we did find this in a trash barrel in the hallway to the rest rooms."

He handed John the guard's jacket Sebastian had spotted earlier. Rats! Sebastian had wanted to be the one to show him. Oh, well, he decided. They were all in this mystery together. As long as it came to John's attention, that was what mattered.

John examined the jacket. "There's a button missing. Did you find it anywhere in that vicinity?" John asked the officer. When the officer said no, John sniffed the two stains. "Some kind of food stain here, and this seems to be makeup on the collar."

Well, now John knew just about what he knew. Sebastian figured he'd better get back to business!

When they were both satisfied that the old grouch was busy picking on somebody else for a change, John said he wanted to talk to the mayor.

"Then you'll have to dance with me," she told him. "If I keep dancing, maybe everyone else will, too."

"Well, er, yes, ma'am," John agreed.

Sebastian crept onto the dance floor to listen. He did his best to wiggle and swing like the others so he wouldn't call attention to himself.

"This is certainly an embarrassment to the city," Mayor Bellows told John as he whirled her around the floor. "It will be a terrible strike against me, too." She nodded to where television floodlights were focused on Patrick Rogers, who was being inter-

viewed. "Look at him! I can just hear Rogers telling the voters that if I can't take care of a time capsule, I certainly shouldn't be in charge of the city."

Sebastian ambled over to the edge of the crowd to eavesdrop. "Why, she can't even take care of a simple time capsule left in her care," Rogers was saying. "How can she take care of a city this size?"

The mayor was right about this man. Had he stolen the time capsule contents in order to embarrass the mayor? If so, he shouldn't be voted into office. And if not, he surely was taking advantage of the situation.

"I came over as soon as I heard about this terrible crime," Patrick Rogers said. "I was out listening to the voters' needs, while the mayor was lending herself to this frivolity."

He hadn't been here? If not, how could he have stolen the capsule contents? Maybe he'd had someone else do the job for him. Then again, he could be lying about his whereabouts.

Rogers was a short, stocky man, almost square. There was no way he could have fit into that jacket, even if he'd wanted to. Any one of the Vander-Vandens could have fit into it, though. It always came back to them.

"As a matter of fact," Rogers continued, "I was at a rally, raising funds for my campaign. I and my hundreds—er, I mean, thousands—of supporters. Thousands of supporters who are tired of this mayor and want a change." He held up his hand to show a bandage. "That's from shaking hands all evening, folks. I never left the rally!"

Sebastian figured pretty soon the guy would need a bandage for his mouth! No need to listen to Rogers anymore. He seemed to have shed all the light he was going to. Sebastian was not dismissing the man as a suspect, but he thought he could put Rogers on the back burner for a while.

Sebastian wanted to get a better look at the time capsule. It was still under wraps on the stage, and two guards were standing by it. But there hadn't been a guard yet who could stop the old sleuth when he wanted to get something.

He strolled around the edge of the room, then worked his way to the back of the stage. The table on which the capsule rested was near the back. As quietly as he could, he crawled up under the satin cover John had thrown over it.

With the spotlight still beaming down on the spot, it was light enough under the cloth for him to get a pretty good look at the box. There it was, still open and as empty as his tummy felt right now. The combination lock and wax lay broken beside it.

And what was that? A single dark black thread was caught on a rusted corner.

Sebastian tasted the thread. It was not cotton or wool or silk. It stretched slightly to his touch. If he was not mistaken (and he rarely was), this was a

45

synthetic blend—polyester. Then it was certainly a modern thread, since polyester was not available in 1929, when the capsule was buried.

What was more, the thread was black, just like Vanessa's catering costume. The evidence was surely mounting against Vanessa. And what was that strange smear on the corner of the box? It glowed in the dark.

Sebastian flicked out his pink tongue to taste the substance. Blah! It was paint of some kind. It must be phosphorus paint. But why would there be paint on the box? Had it been there all these years? Or had it rubbed off from the thief? Maybe from his costume? Was anyone dressed like a glow-in-the-dark Halloween ghost? No, all these costumes were from the twenties. He would have to let his keen mind think about this awhile.

Sebastian didn't want to dismiss the other VanderVandens, who were an odd lot. It seemed the only one not under suspicion was Vanoise VanderVanden, alias Van Hamlet, since he wasn't there—or was he?

Sebastian knew he needed to look casual as he continued his investigation, eavesdropping on the police interviews. And what looked casual here? Dancing and eating. Since he obviously couldn't ask anyone to dance, he thought he'd best go through the food line.

One of the waiters in his tall chef's hat—actually,

that fellow who'd been talking with Vanessa earlier—stood behind the serving table and filled the people's plates as they passed by. Sebastian placed his front paws on the table and nudged his plate toward the man, squinting to get a good look at his name badge. It said "Dashiel."

Dashiel put one, two, then three slices of roast beef on Sebastian's plate. The hungry hawkshaw didn't move on.

"Sir?" the waiter said in an irritable tone. "More?" He added two more pieces. "There are also vegetables, sir. You do want to leave room on your plate for vegetables, don't you, sir?"

Not particularly. But Sebastian chose to move on rather than cause a scene that would call attention to himself. Vanessa had finished her interview and was serving behind the table, too, although she kept glancing around nervously. Was she afraid of being caught as the thief, or was she trying to avoid another confrontation with her aunt?

Sebastian eyed her uniform as she waited on him, piling on mashed potatoes and broccoli. There was a small snag on the vest, where her name tag had been pinned and pulled out many times. And it looked as if an entire line of weave was gone. Had he found the missing thread at the scene of the crime? He hated to admit it, but all the evidence pointed to Vanessa.

Sebastian moved behind the table. The waiter had

a snag on his trousers, too. The material these uniforms were made out of didn't seem very sturdy. Of course, the waiter wasn't really a suspect, although he might have stolen the items to sell.

What had the man's tag said his name was? Dashiel. And Sebastian had overheard him telling an officer his last name was York. Dashiel York? An odd name, it sounded made up. Of course, no odder than the VanderVanden combinations.

Combination? The word hit his brain like a hammer. Quickly he glanced at the pictures on the wall. Just as he'd thought! Why hadn't he noticed before? The time capsule box under the cloth had a combination lock. The one in the picture, the one that had been in the cornerstone, had a padlock!

7
Solutions Taste Better Dipped in Gravy

Sebastian's mind raced on fast forward, sifting facts. What if the box, as well as the lock, were different? Sebastian trotted closer to the picture. The blowup was so clear that he could make out the manufacturer's number on the box. 093028/Tor Mfg. That meant that Tor Manufacturing had turned out this particular model in September of 1928.

Detecting gave him a real appetite, Sebastian suddenly realized! He gobbled down the roast beef and potatoes, leaving the broccoli, then dashed behind the stage once more. Nosing up under the cloth, he read: 020286/Spartan Mfg.

While the boxes were almost identical, this was most certainly not the same box that had been buried sixty years ago. And it certainly didn't have the same lock.

Clearly an almost identical box had been substituted for the real one. And probably when the lights were out earlier. It had to have been then, the only time the box had been out of sight.

What if Sebastian had turned his own master mind toward criminal activities instead of toward defeating criminals? How would he have performed this particular crime? he asked himself.

He would have disguised himself as a guard and tried to remove and then put back the real capsule. And if that didn't work, he'd have tried to substitute a like box for the real one. Perhaps he'd have hidden the phony box nearby. It was small enough to fit almost anywhere. The thief could have stashed it somewhere, and while the lights were out, switched them, sneaking away with the real box when the coast was clear, probably even before the theft had been discovered. Still, how would he have gotten the box out from under their very eyes, especially with the lights out only a minute or so? Too, the thief would have had to be at the ballroom early. And who could have been here early? Once again, the evidence pointed to Vanessa. She was the only person with a motive who could have done that. Or was she?

So, Vanessa had the motive. She thought she could sell the contents of the capsule to collectors and make enough to put herself through college, if her father disinherited her. She had the opportunity, since she was definitely here early, helping to set up the buffet. And she had the means, since she could easily disguise herself as a guard, spirit away the box, and blend back into the crowd of waiters again. The jacket would have been a bit large, but it was possible that no one would have noticed.

Sebastian and the musicians had arrived within an hour of the incident when the lights went out, and Vanessa was at work. Either she was innocent, then, or she hadn't had the chance to leave with the real time capsule. If she was guilty, the time capsule had to be here. But where? The officer said they'd looked everywhere in the building, and they probably had.

Maybe the officers hadn't looked in the more obvious places! Sebastian scooted over the dance floor, between legs, to the buffet table. Maybe she'd hidden it under the table, or in one of the carts.

He slipped under the table, but, no, there was nothing there. All he could see were shoes, smaller ones that must belong to Vanessa and larger ones that must belong to Dashiel York. As the bigger shoes moved, Sebastian caught a glint of gold. Just a hint, and for only a moment. What had he seen? He needed to know more.

Although it was only a quick glance, Sebastian was sure that the glint had come from the cuff of the man's trousers. Sebastian moved closer and peered inside. It was a button, a gold button. And it had SASA engraved on it. It had to be the button missing from the guard's uniform, and it was in

Dashiel's trouser cuff. And that, in turn, had to mean that it had been Dashiel and not Vanessa who'd worn the guard's jacket.

But why would Dashiel have committed the crime? And, if he had, why hadn't he left with the box before the theft had been discovered? He could have pretended to be sick or made another excuse to leave. Unless he had a reason for staying. But what?

Sebastian looked up. He saw John going toward the stage to interview the guard who was on duty and followed him as closely as possible.

"Can you describe the fellow you say was here when the lights went out?" John asked him.

"Yes, sir!" the guard replied. "He was approximately five feet, eleven inches. He was of medium weight, probably a hundred and sixty pounds. He had sort of graying strawberry blond hair and brown eyes."

Van VanderVanden III had graying strawberry blond hair, Sebastian remembered. He also had a motive, since he had not been allowed to buy the capsule. But he didn't have brown eyes. It was Dashiel who had brown eyes and was about the height and weight the security guard had described. Of course, he didn't have graying strawberry blond hair. Unless . . .

What if Dashiel had worn a graying strawberry blond wig? Sebastian wiggled with excitement. His solution was almost perfect! He remembered Vanessa saying earlier that the waiter had pushed the squeaky cart over and offered the guard some food.

What if he'd stashed the fake time capsule on the cart and wheeled the cart near the stage? He might have moved that box from the cart to under the table. That wouldn't have been hard. Nobody was paying attention to the waiters. And since the table's cloth cover went all the way to the floor, it could easily have concealed a second box. What if he'd waited until the lights went out, then switched boxes in the dark? Did that mean he had an accomplice? Was Vanessa part of this, after all? There was the makeup on the uniform jacket. And who but a woman would wear makeup?

No, Vanessa was much shorter than five-eleven. She could not disguise her height. If he could just get John to see the gold button. John already knew about the jacket. He could figure out the rest—with the cagey canine's help, of course. In a flash, Sebastian leaped onto the stage, snatched John's notebook, and made a mad dash for the waiter with John in pursuit, yelling things Sebastian would not dare repeat.

He tried his best to stop, but smacked into Dashiel, and the two of them toppled to the floor. In an instant, the gold button spilled from the pants cuff, Dashiel's short brush mustache moved over to his cheek, and his thick black hair fell to the floor, revealing graying strawberry blond hair. And to top it all, one brown contact lens popped out, revealing a familiar emerald green.

"Uncle Vanoise!" Vanessa squealed. "It's you!"

Vanoise, the actor? That would explain the makeup, or greasepaint. And it would also explain the phosphorus smear on the box. In the theater, actors used those marks to find their proper places on a darkened stage. He'd marked the box so he could find it when the lights went out!

Vanoise VanderVanden staggered to his feet and took off, running toward the service exit. Vanessa ran after him, yelling. John took off after them both.

VanderVandens, who were running about and yelling, gave chase, too. And Sebastian, not about to miss out on the finale, dashed after them all.

He caught up with them in a heap at the service entrance, where the Downtown Catering Company truck was parked.

"Look!" Vanita VanderVanden was shouting. She emerged from the catering truck, dripping in roast beef and gravy. And she was carrying the rusty metal box with the padlock. "I found it! Look, Van II! Look, Van III! Look, Vanessa! I found the time capsule!"

He had stashed the box under the dome with the roast beef, just as Sebastian had suspected.

"Why did you take the time capsule, Vanoise?" the doddering Van II was demanding. Sebastian noted that the VanderVandens were all talking at

once and to each other for a change.

"This has been worth it," Vanoise said finally. "If it will bring us together to talk for a change, then I'll take my punishment."

He told them how he'd managed to take the box, and it was pretty much the way Sebastian had figured out.

Vanoise had played two roles tonight. He was the waiter Dashiel York and the unnamed security guard. Earlier, he'd wheeled the fake box behind the stage, hidden under the dome of a food warmer. He'd given the guard some of the food, then made an excuse to leave the cart there for a while.

Hurrying to the rest room, he'd put on the SASA

jacket and returned as a guard, without his black wig and mustache but with his brown contact lenses still in place.

He had put a timer on the fuse box to make it short out for a minute or two, long enough to switch the metal boxes. Then he'd rushed out and taken off the guard jacket and, in his haste, unknowingly torn the telltale button from the jacket.

Later, again in his wig and mustache, he'd returned and wheeled away the cart, with the real time capsule in it beside the roast beef. He'd secreted it in the catering van before the theft had been discovered.

He hadn't left the ball, of course, because he'd

wanted to see the reaction of his siblings when they discovered the items were missing.

"I would never have sold those things. Some of them were our toys when we were children and liked each other—*sometimes*. I just wanted to embarrass them the way they've embarrassed me," Vanoise, alias Van Hamlet, said, moaning. It may have been his best performance ever. "I would have returned it, honestly. I contributed to that capsule, too. Those cat's-eye marbles were mine. But I wasn't even asked to the ball! I just wanted *them* to suffer a little, too."

Since the items were recovered and were auctioned for a tidy sum, the mayor decided to drop charges against Vanoise. And when Sebastian left the convention center, all the VanderVandens— even Vanessa—were yelling at one another, but at least they were communicating. Maybe they could work out their problems. Sebastian hoped so.

As for his own problems, Sebastian dashed to the costume shop and shoved the costume through the night return slot in the door—not before removing John's credit card, of course. Scurrying home as quickly as he could, Sebastian put the card back on John's dresser. Whew! Not a toothprint on it. He raced into the living room and took a flying leap onto the couch.

He had just shut his eyes when John opened the door. "Look at you, lazy dog!" John teased. "I do believe you'd sleep right through a burglary—unless they tried to steal the couch."

Yawning to keep up his little charade, Sebastian wiggled his stump of a tail and followed John into the bedroom.

"Boy, am I beat!" John muttered as he shed his costume. He put on his pajamas, keeping up a constant banter with Sebastian. "You'd never believe what a night I've had, old fellow. You could say I have good news and bad news."

Sebastian cocked his head, waiting for more information. The good news would be that he solved the case. But the bad news?

John reached down and rubbed Sebastian under the chin. "I cracked a case. I guess it would've been a lot harder if that weird fellow hadn't grabbed my notebook and taken off with it. Officer Daniel said his name was Roy Arp, I think. Odd fellow."

No credit again! The very idea! Sebastian sauntered off to the kitchen to find a snack that would soothe away the insults John had hurled. Besides, it had been hours since he'd eaten. And solving cases made him hungry.

John was sitting on the side of the bed when Sebastian returned from his snack: his semi-yummy dog food plus half a loaf of bread John had carelessly left out on the cabinet. John pulled off one of his socks and threw it under the bed. "I was feeling so good, in fact, that I asked Maude to marry me."

"Hack, hack!" Sebastian choked on his doggie yummy. *That* was the bad news!

"She said no, old fellow. She said she just wasn't ready for marriage yet."

Sebastian stuck his cold nose in John's hand and licked it sympathetically. Inside he was happy because he'd still have John to himself. But he was a bit sad, too, because John seemed sad. Who did Maude think she was, anyway, turning them down? She'd never do better than handsome John and his clever, fuzzy sidekick!

John threw his other sock under the bed. "Well, she didn't say *never*, old fellow. She just said not yet. I guess there's still hope, huh?"

Sure, but were they hoping for the same thing?

"And, meanwhile, there are still the bad guys to track down, right?"

Sebastian rolled over and kicked all four feet in the air. Right. And he, Sebastian (Super Sleuth), sure felt that was something to look forward to.

"All in all, we don't have a bad life, wouldn't you say?" John asked, reaching down to tickle Sebastian's exposed tummy.

Sebastian jumped up and ran to find his ball, wagging his tail as he did. Ball wasn't his favorite game, but it always seemed to cheer John up.

His human was right, he knew. It was not a bad life at all!